The Case of the Missing Duckie

by Linda Hayward • Illustrated by Maggie Swanson

Featuring Jim Henson's Sesame Street Muppets

A SESAME STREET/GOLDEN PRESS BOOK
Published by Western Publishing Company, Inc.
in conjunction with Children's Television Workshop.

The day the duckie disappeared was Ernie's birthday.
Because it was a special day, Ernie had decided to
spend it doing things he liked to do. And the thing he
liked to do most was take a bath with his Rubber Duckie.

Right after breakfast Ernie went into the bathroom
and filled the bathtub with water. He put a brand-new bar
of soap in the soap dish and he hung a soft, fluffy towel
on the towel rack.

Ernie picked up Rubber Duckie and gave him a little squeeze.

"You know, Rubber Duckie," he said, "you are my very best friend. I could never take a bath without you. Who would I talk to if I felt lonely? Who would cheer me up if I got soapsuds in my eye? Gee, Rubber Duckie, I'm awfully fond of you."

Just then the telephone rang and Ernie went
to answer it. "I bet someone is calling to wish me
Happy Birthday," he thought.
He left Rubber Duckie on the stool in the bathroom.

"Hello?"

"Hi, Ernie! This is Big Bird. I just called to ask you a question. Are you going to be home at two o'clock this afternoon?"

"Gee, Big Bird, I guess so," said Ernie. "What is happening at two o'clock this afternoon?"

"Oh, nothing," said Big Bird. "I was just wondering if you were going to be home then, that's all. Well, good-bye, Ernie."

"Hmmm. Big Bird didn't wish me Happy Birthday," thought Ernie. "Maybe he doesn't know that today is my birthday. Gee, maybe no one knows that today is my birthday. Oh, well, I still have Rubber Duckie to keep me company."

When Ernie returned to the bathroom, he had
a strange feeling that something was missing.

"Now what could be missing?" he said.
"I remembered the soap. I remembered the towel.
Rubber Duckie, what did I forget? Rubber Duckie?
RUBBER DUCKIE?!"

Ernie stared at the stool where he had left Rubber
Duckie.

Rubber Duckie was gone!

Ernie went back to the telephone.

He called his friend Sherlock Hemlock the detective.

"Hello, Mr. Hemlock," said Ernie. "Something terrible has happened. I need a detective."

"I'll be there in a minute," said Sherlock Hemlock.

A minute later there was a knock on the front door and Ernie opened it.

"It is I, Sherlock Hemlock, the world's greatest detective," said the man with the magnifying glass. "What seems to be the trouble?"

"I was going to take a bath when I noticed that something was missing," said Ernie.

Sherlock looked at Ernie very carefully.

"Aha! I have it!" he cried. "Your clothes are missing!"

"My clothes are in the bathroom," Ernie explained.

"Then I will begin looking for your clothes in the bathroom," said Sherlock.

Ernie followed Sherlock Hemlock into the bathroom.

"Gadzooks! I have found the missing clothes," cried Sherlock.

"But my clothes were never missing," said Ernie. "The thing that is missing is..."

"The soap!" said Sherlock.

"No, not the soap," said Ernie. "The soap is right here. It is..."

"The bathtub!" cried Sherlock.

"No, no, not the bathtub," said Ernie. "It is Rubber Duckie that is missing."

"Of course!" said Sherlock. "Now I understand.
It all fits together...the soap, the bathtub, the towel
hanging on the towel rack. You were about to wash
dishes when..."

"I was about to take a bath," said Ernie.

"You were about to take a bath," said Sherlock,
"when your rubber guppy jumped out of the water..."

"No, it wasn't a rubber guppy," said Ernie.

"Rubber puppy? Ruffled buggy? Dubby nucky?" said
Sherlock in a puzzled sort of way.

Ernie sighed sadly.

"It's a cute, chubby little fellow named Rubber Duckie who is missing," said Ernie. "He disappeared while I was in the living room answering the telephone."

"In that case," said Sherlock, "I shall call this case 'The Case of the Missing Duckie'! And I shall begin solving this case by looking for clues in the living room."

"Let me tell you about clues, Ernie," said Sherlock,
as he inspected the telephone. "A clue can be as small
as a scrap of paper or a piece of thread or a speck of
dust."

Sherlock looked in the wastepaper basket.
He picked up a pincushion.
He lifted the corner of the rug.

Sherlock opened the closet door and poked around
inside.

"A clue can be something so tiny that no one but
a detective would notice it..." he told Ernie.

But Ernie did not hear Sherlock. He was on his way
back to the bathroom to take his bath.

"I guess I'll just...sit in the bathtub and...look
at the faucet and...talk to the soap and...ohhh,
what am I going to do without (sniff)...Rubber
(sniff, sniff)...Duckie?"

But Sherlock did not hear Ernie. He was still looking for a clue.

"And I, Sherlock Hemlock, the world's greatest detective, will go on searching for the missing rubber... the missing rubber... now what was it that I shall go on searching for?" asked Sherlock Hemlock.

Ten minutes later Ernie was still sitting in the bathtub, staring at the faucet and feeling very sad — because there is nothing sadder than being sad on your birthday — when Sherlock popped in, carrying a big box full of rubber bands.

"The Case of the Missing Rubber Bands is solved!" said Sherlock.

"Gee, Mr. Hemlock," said Ernie. "That's Bert's rubber band collection. His rubber band collection isn't missing."

As Ernie was drying off, Sherlock stuck his head
in the bathroom again.

"Here it is!" he cried. "The missing rubber plant!"

"That's Bert's rubber plant," said Ernie. "I didn't
lose a rubber plant. How could I take a bath with
a rubber plant?"

Ernie was just putting on his shirt when Sherlock appeared again. Sherlock's arms were full.

"I, Sherlock Hemlock, have found the missing rubber ball, the missing rubber raft, the missing rubber glove, and the missing rubber stamp."

"I'm sorry, Mr. Hemlock," said Ernie, "but none of those things is missing."

Just then Bert came into the bathroom.

"Hey, Ern," he said, "have you seen my rubber stamp, my rubber glove, my rubber raft, my rubber ball, my rubber plant, and my rubber bands? They are all missing."

"Everything is here in the bathroom, Bert," said Ernie. "Everything (sniff) except Rubber Duckie."

"Egad!" cried Sherlock. "Don't tell me that Rubber Duckie is missing, too!"

Finally Sherlock decided to stop searching for clues
in Bert's room and went into the kitchen.

"Gadzooks!" he cried as he examined the wall.
"Green fingerprints! Pink fingerprints! Yellow
fingerprints! This can mean only one thing! Some green,
pink, and yellow monsters stole Rubber Duckie!"

Sherlock decided to hide in the living room closet
and wait for the green, pink, and yellow monsters
to return.

At two o'clock in the afternoon the doorbell rang
and Ernie went to see who was there.

Everybody was there!

"Surprise!" they all shouted.

"We brought you a birthday party," said Big Bird.
"That's why I wanted to know if you would be here
at two o'clock."

It was a wonderful birthday party. There were presents and lots of big, fat balloons — green balloons, pink balloons, yellow balloons.

"Zounds!" cried Sherlock, as he opened the closet door and walked — BOP! — right into a bunch of balloons. "I have found the green and pink and yellow monsters!"

"No, Mr. Hemlock. Those are balloons for Ernie's birthday party," said Big Bird.

"Aha! I have it! These are balloons for Ernie's birthday party," said Sherlock.

"If only Rubber Duckie could be here," said Ernie. "He likes birthday parties, too."

"Don't worry, Ernest. I, Sherlock Hemlock, will soon solve The Case of the Missing Duckie. But first— I must solve The Case of the Missing Cake. If this is a birthday party, where is the birthday cake?"

The kitchen door opened and Cookie Monster came out carrying a big birthday cake covered with green and pink and yellow frosting.

And right in the middle of the frosting sat . . .

"Rubber Duckie!" cried Ernie. "Am I glad to see you!"

"HAPPY BIRTHDAY, DEAR ERNIE . . ." sang everyone, "HAPPY BIRTHDAY TO YOU!"

"Me borrow Rubber Duckie for birthday cake,"
said Cookie Monster.

"Aha!" cried Sherlock. "I have it! Cookie Monster
borrowed Rubber Duckie for the birthday cake. I,
Sherlock Hemlock, have solved yet another cake . . . I
mean, case."